Old Man River

by

Jill Strafford

Grosvenor House
Publishing Limited

This book is published by
Grosvenor House Publishing Ltd
Link House
140 The Broadway, Tolworth, Surrey, KT6 7HT.
www.grosvenorhousepublishing.co.uk

This book is a work of fiction. Any resemblance to
people or events, past or present, is purely coincidental.

A CIP record for this book
is available from the British Library

ISBN 978-1-83975-605-4

DEDICATION

This book is for my husband Mick, who has shown me so much support and given me endless freedom to be able to write this book.

PROLOGUE

Three women boarded a train on the same day, at the same time. There were just three carriages, and each woman sat separately, unaware their kindred spirits were not far away, each in a different carriage.

SERA

Sera sat by the window in coach one and gazed out at the grey platform, the grey weather and the grey people, all huddled together in a mist of gauze. This train was particularly splendid, it was very new and had a welcoming scent about it; it felt like one had arrived.

There was also a stillness about the train, a quiet, unassuming stillness, where there was somehow a different air to breathe, something soothing.

Looking out of the window, she felt that real sense of leaving somewhere that no longer had a hold on her and going towards somewhere that was new and exciting. Her favourite place was being in the middle of the two, she was in neither one place or another, as there was no responsibility, no hold, nothing but moving forward and enjoying every single moment of not being needed by anyone or anything.

With this recipe of necessity, there had to be a good read at hand – and three cups of coffee in a row without judgement from anyone, the questions, the contempt, the look of horror that she could drink that much coffee in one hour from her onlookers, followed by, 'Do you sleep at night?'

Then she would find herself saying, 'I only have single shots, and I drink two litres of water a day,' adding, with a rush of anger at their judgement, 'Of course I sleep at night as I make sure to knock myself out with as many gins as I desire.'

Here on the train, with no one to ruffle her feathers, she let out a breath of relief and took in the luxury of nothing, nothing at all.

Sera looked down at the sparkle of her ruby ring and relished the light that danced on the three stones, she delighted in the display of colour, she craved colour, particularly from the outdoor world, it fell like a blanket of trust around her shoulders, reminding her of life yet to come.

She placed her hot cup of coffee on the table and lost herself in thought.

She was looking up at the same small speck of blue sky that she saw for the first time in her fragile life, probably age three and a half, a blue so blue it stayed in her veins forever. Laughter so light she felt the dance beneath her bones so young. There was fragility and splendour; her eyes became alive for the first time, the wonderment and merriment too soon gone.

Sera saw her legs holding onto the shoulders of he who would carry her for a few moments and in these moments show her security and stability. Her mother was holding the hand of her small brother, laughter was chuckling downstream, and the birds were singing triumphantly in her new world.

Unfortunately, this wasn't going to last for long, this joy, this new-found joy. She didn't ask any questions as she never thought to; life just moved on. There was a feeling of going from place to place for a while, which is where she met the grey. She never felt particularly well, her clothes were dreary and often itched. So began the feeling of never being good enough, because she obviously didn't deserve it. Nothing was held together, nothing made sense. Her mother was her magnet to anything at all, it was all she had to hold herself to, this is who she followed, all she knew for any type of survival.

Now, looking through the window of the good house, where the good children live, she saw an angelic-looking little girl, all made up of loveliness, she wore pretty clothes, with colours of the softest reds. She was surrounded by gentle voices, she played with her dolls house, with its real twinkly lights and red chimney pot. Sera looks more closely at herself and sees a pauper of a girl, a little match girl, trying to keep warm by the warmth of the good house and the good girl. But the good girl didn't see Sera, she wasn't interested in the outside, content within her gentle world, where there were no wars and no hatred.

So, Sera turned and walked away towards the forest that beckoned and folded over her blue body to reshape her back into chaos and noise. There was no gentleness there, apart from the smile of a mother that waited to bring her back to life one day. The feathers flew and led her to mirrors that reflected all things heavenly; she pocketed this in her heart and looked for further treasures to lift the senses.

3

Back in her present, Sera saw the vastness of sky outside, and the most beautiful building in the distance, which shone like mirrors and reflected light into her heart, bringing tears to her eyes. She couldn't believe she hadn't noticed this before.

There was a silence about the train that lulled her to rest; she actually felt secure, which was so unusual for her that she allowed herself to relish in it. There were countless occasions in her life where she thought someone was behind her, it was very unnerving, and survival instincts kicked in on a daily basis – was there really someone there? Was it a spirit? Was it a warning? But for some reason, this train trip was very different, there was no fear, and this was clearly a desirable way forward.

A larger-than-life conductor arrived in her carriage quite out of the blue. He was all aglow with humour and joy; he carried a book in one hand and a silver wand type thing in the other, leaving no hands left for reaching into his conductor's bag.

'Hello, miss,' he chimed.

'Hello,' she said happily. She noted what he was carrying and couldn't help but ask, 'What book are you reading? I noticed the picture on the front, it reminds me of that beautiful building we just passed, and I didn't even know existed.'

'It's *The Hidden Life of Trees*.' He showed her the cover. 'Have you read it?'

'Yes, yes, I have. It's a beautiful book. At the moment I'm reading a Ben Okri book, A Time For A new Dream'

'Ben Okri,' he said with vigour.

'Yes, you know him?'

'I certainly do, miss. I know him very well.'

'You really know him?'

'I really know him… but now I need to attend to this.' And he showed her his e-cigarette. 'Yes, it's all about mathematics is this, and I need to work it out. There's a fella waiting for me in the next cabin who can help me, but he doesn't know it yet.' He laughed out loud and went on his way.

Sera felt lifted and a little fizzy with excitement regarding her journey

Sera was thinking of a song, 'A Passenger' by Iggy Pop. The words were replaying over and over in her head. She had felt so tired of riding this planet; it had become like a merry-go-round that had lost its magic, and the tinkling music that lost its tinkle in some seedy seaside resort, full of empty crisp packets, dog poo, sticky sweets, screaming kids and screaming adults, complaining and repeating the same old nothings. She had tried to cling onto happiness when it arrived – as happiness was fleeting, she was precious about it when it was there – but already feeling the loss of it before it had even gone.

This, though, felt like a magical train trip, as if seeds of sensuous sippings were being remembered, from past and present, all things bright. It was the train you dreamed about that takes you to new lands and incredible shorelines. The all-seeing face, observing the light in the flower, seeing heaven in the white bud, swimming in the green, and swimming in the blue, there seemed to be a whole new world of colour.

She knew how the thread running through all life brought certain people and events together, like a huge tapestry, ready to be worked upon, give colour, take colour, placed and replaced, sewn and left undone, always loved. The thread that brought the earthlings together was no coincidence. The spirit of air running from the dark, running from gateway to gateway to find a force of light streaming through every crevice, and every lost place, where stagnation had found its home.

Thus, Sera was a writer, she wrote stories told by shadows and whirlwinds, messages heard from ancestors, and Spirit, by the presence she felt behind her, the sounds of nature, the woodland and all who lived there, and in the simple patterns of life… There was one particular day when she felt the wind, still but adamant, push her in the direction of the house by the river. Against her better judgement, she gathered her wellies, her snuggly coat and her keys and off she went, feeling great apprehension and excitement.

Rosebuds of deepest purest reds submerged and gathered in baby baskets, waiting to lift burdens of heavy dew in the early morning of the new beginning. The trees whispered in another language, the feeling of wealth as she swam through the golden green, freedom of spirit and life beyond, the lull to sleep beneath the great Eucalyptus tree that had been planted on the mountain. Misty youth, broken pots, dusty bikes, drinking adults, money and wealth, it all exploded with a quality of life, and it sang its heart out as its story was ready to be held in the hearts of those who heard. Oh, how sweet was the art of the gesture of life. Her story had to continue, and maybe she would find the answer in the jewels of the wood.

As Sera arrived at the barbed wire gate, she felt the sickness in her stomach that was always there to warn her to back off. It would find its way to the roof of her mouth, where the soft palate was, it would pulse very slowly, she would go quiet and listen carefully. But not this day. She was greedy for jewels, and that was all she could see. One step through the wired gate, and she had begun her journey. Her heart pounded furiously, she looked and looked for anything she could borrow for her story, anything at all.

There didn't seem to be anyone around, which was good. She approached the doorless door frame and glared at the horror of the once-loved house, now tortured and dishonoured. There was the sound of a dog barking in the distance, making her jump, and she was scared as she quietly stepped in, desperately trying to think of reasons to explain why she was trespassing if she were to be approached.

Above what was once the hearth, she could see a dark mirror, silvery black in colour – one of the things she came for. She needed this, it was perfection, it took her down tunnels, the tunnels beneath ground, where the roots built cities. As she placed her fingers gently on the blackberry glass, she felt the very same roots grab her feet, she saw the jewels she had borrowed fall to the ground and pulled in by the earth, the heavy earth stealing her life, her breath and her story.

Life as Sera knew it ceased in that moment, all that was left were bones and blood, ready for the deep underground and to find their way back to life through the branches of the trees where the birds sang their hearts out, telling the world of the misfortunes of others. But no one heard, no one. That song was wasted upon human ears.

INDIA

India sat excitedly by the window in her amazing carriage, the middle one. The train appeared empty, which was good news as she could spread out a bit, her tea on the table, her earphones at the ready. Even her book made up of rich words and colours, her inner world was so exciting to her, and there was so much to do all the time.

Nothing could ever be the same; she lived in several different worlds. To the onlooker, she looked like a normal person who tinkled around doing her thing. There was an air of wild and free around her, her colours were grounding. She loved the Romany ways: their frayed edges, the smell of log fires burning, telling of wonderful and exciting stories; of scents of sandalwood, feather quilts, red ripped skirts, twisting round and round with the dancer; of laughter, rolled up cigarettes, wild parties with drunk and ravishing women stripped to the waist and searching for love or amusement from men sitting at the ready, for a woman to fall into their arms to dance or be ravished.

India was eager to explore from within; she gained her strength this way.

She sat admiring the trinity ring that she wore on her thumb. It shone brightly as the golden sun poured through the train window, made of a quality that never seemed to age, passed down to her from her gran. India loved the idea that the ring supported her, as it had her mother and her grandmother.

Her thoughts were interrupted by the sound of a man's voice, joyful and melodic. It was the conductor, who beamed a huge smile at her. His eyes twinkled, he looked like a man you could trust. She began rooting for her ticket.

'It's alright, miss,' he said. 'You look like a person I can trust. I'm very sure you have that ticket somewhere around. Do you know where you're headed to?'

'Yes,' India said, and then, 'Erm no… I can't remember right now.' She felt a little alarmed. 'It's on the tip of my tongue.'

'No matter,' he bellowed happily. 'When you remember, you can tell me.'

She was so relieved; the heat rising in her body began to dissipate.

'Enjoy the rest of your trip,' he said as he began leaving her side.

'Oh – do you serve drinks?'

'Yes, but we only have spirits on board,' he roared happily.

'I just wanted tea,' India said, but he'd passed by then, and she decided to await his return.

As she gazed out of the window, she couldn't believe how blue the sky was; it reminded her of the 'lockdown' due to the Covid-19 virus. As she'd not before had time in her life to really look at what was around her, she was overwhelmed with the colour and splendour she'd missed in her own back garden, along with the quiet and peace.

The golden warmth of the sun made her feel fully alive and awake, and she rummaged around in her bag for a book to read: *The Vision: Reflections on the Way of the Soul* by Kahlil Gibran. She held it lovingly in her two hands when all of a sudden, she felt a pain in her heart, it came with force and left as soon as it arrived. She put her hands on the table to steady herself.

'Here you are, miss, that warming cuppa you asked for, thought you might need it.'

She looked up in astonishment; she hadn't heard the conductor approach. She thanked him profusely.

'Ooh, excellent choice of literature there.' He grinned. 'Now you enjoy your tea and your book, and I'll be back later

India picked up her book, had a sip of her tea, and felt better. She opened the book on page three. Her spirit soared

India was swimming in the blue. Her spirit was laden with sunlit lavender, sparkling radiant roots, twisted and gnarled like knuckles dripping into the blue/green water, dipping deeper, rearing a new breath, finding its way to underground life, descent and loss, loss finding its way back to new life, and lifting to the surface like a gentle twist of spirit smoke, finding its way through bubble and back to air to then circulate in a spiral motion of foreverness. A damp lust lay in the warm brown land, confiscating death, adoring green shoots and new beginnings, always, always in love with the maker of life, the mother and father of our first breath:

Send us to the stars, let our hearts yearn for tranquil chills, India's spirit sang out, destiny drawing us back to our ancestors, and upwards to our maker, or dreams. Taking us beyond our bridges, the further we ride on the backs of horses, the further we gallop away from chaos.

The lioness is heard, she calls out to the Magus, to the Gods and the Goddesses, she prowls and ponders, carefully, carelessly, wanting and unwanting. Living and breathing, she hears the story, she addresses the story, delivers the story. And spares all life of its vulnerability, well in this time and space anyway.

The music of the living eases out of the mouths of the listeners; they perch on the waves by the shores and allow themselves to be transported into the melodic spheres...

In the depths of this interior world, India passed through roots and rubble; every now and again, she would feel the pull of certain roots, pulling her back in time or forward in time, she wasn't sure. She had been enjoying life in the green of the mossy woods, looking for things she couldn't quite see; she found bones in the ancient burial ground, she saw them being dug beneath, the death of the bones was a treacherous and cruel death, the possibility of slaughter.

India felt the desire to throw up, took her leave, moved on. She saw a city hidden by the quarry walls, life was busy building and progressing, candles were lit, and trolls protected the outskirts, rearing their ugliness above ground to frighten off any earth being. India loved this as she could see it all, but again took her leave hastily, only to find a vortex in the damp moss – this was an energy of the world of electrolytes; mineral beings used it as a gateway to earth and back.

As she was roaming around the great vortex, she was being watched tentatively.

Anupa and Bhavani arrived through this channel, called by the fawn men. Anupa and Bhavani were the colour and appearance of a bubble film, their feminine energy showed in grace and movement, their form was simple and elegant, gentle doe eyes, lights within were illuminating their surroundings with a soft, friendly glow. Anupa hid behind Grandmother tree, and Bhavani behind Grandfather tree. Anupa carried with her an empty bottle, she wanted to fill it with the jewels of the earth, and she watched India as she entered the gateway to the golden cathedral, she couldn't see her clearly in the earthly light, but as she entered the gates, India was surrounded by heavenly light.

The fawn men were their guardians, as Anupa and Bhavani were vulnerable beings, trusting and hungry for knowledge. They looked upon

India with intrigue and compassion. The fawn men had spied India in the wooded land and watched her cautiously at first – but seeing her light and her life looking for worlds within and without, they saw her thirst for the knowledge only the wooded area could give. Ballantyne, the leader of the fawn men, had called upon our two electrolytes on midsummer day, he lit fires to honour them and keep away predators; the sun shone upon all involved this joyous day.

Ballantyne's horse was aglow with inner fire and stood mighty and noble, his name was Baal, and he was magnificent. He was regal and possessed great wisdom of the mighty and gallant horse line.

Baal and Ballantyne were as one greatly respected and had lived for thousands of years.

India stood stock still as she felt the strong presence of all these beings, she didn't move a muscle. Anupa approached her and looked deep inside her eyes, she saw light and felt trust for this earthling; India could just see her standing incredibly close and wanted to laugh, she reached up with her arms to welcome this world around her, she saw Ballantyne on his horse, she had seen him before, her fear of this great woodland lord had banished. She felt great love and admiration for this spirit being, she then saw his tribe of fawn men behind all looking on with a fondness toward their new find.

Anupa touched her heart and the crown of her head, then India lost her balance and fell sobbing to the ground.

India soared upwards and out of her body.

SASKIA

Saskia sat by her window in carriage three, a chill of excitement running through her as she put her ice-cold G&T on the table, together with her book by Anne Hamilton called *A Blonde Bengali Wife*, which she was really looking forward to reading.

Oh, this woman, Saskia, knew how to live once upon a time, before the sadness. She felt she needed the right man, a soulmate. She and her husband had a boy together, but she was just waiting for her son to reach 18, and then she planned to leave. Go to visit Bengal and other places she had on her list. She wanted to inspire and be inspired. Her husband had always held her back as she had her duties to uphold before her adventures.

She was remembering years and years ago when life was ripe and rich, days before she left her husband, she was sitting on the sun-laden lawn whilst playing *Songs of the Auvergne*, filling the garden with spirit. Scented flowers were scattered in all corners, baskets of dead flower heads, too. A jug of aperitif was dashed with borage flowers; salads ladened with nasturtiums grew by the lilac tree.

Now Saskia was dreaming of frost and snow, gleaming and glowing while the sun smacked a decision to grant the purest white light, with blinding blizzards and sleet, of snow crystals – all in her deep blue eyes. She saw the sweetness of the frozen snowflake, its perfect pattern, the glow of the sun touching the surface, holding its head high, shoulders back, proud as you like. Then the sound of cold, shocking laughter, shaking the roots of the soul.

There was confusion inside her, like she'd got out of the wrong side of the bed and put everything on back to front. She also felt cold inside, shivering a little, as if she'd had flu, but there was a separation from one need to another, never thinking for a second that she needed warming up, just this continuation of being cold and wanting cold.

From the next carriage, Saskia heard the joyous sounds of a man's voice, and then the conductor entered her carriage, a very tall African American, who chimed his way towards her.

'Hello, miss,' he said in a kindly fashion. She noticed his name tag, he was called Michael, and it suited him. 'How are you this joyful and most wonderful day?' he asked.

'I'm okay, thank you, I think.' She found herself laughing her nervous laugh.

'Well, please let me know if there's anything you need.' He began his journey away from her.

'Do you need to see my ticket?' she asked. 'And have you got any iced tea?' But he didn't seem to hear, which was a good job, as she couldn't find her ticket anywhere. It might have been because her hands were cold; she was feeling clumsy with it, maybe a hot cuppa would be more appropriate. She'd ask him if Michael passed her again, she hoped he would as she liked him, she liked his warmth.

Saskia stared out of the window, remembering something a little sad. From the age of four, she'd seemed to lose her identity – or maybe it was the world that shaped her this way? She remembered how her mother told her to sit by herself whilst she read her a story. No cuddles or closeness, never the bedtime stories written by gentlefolk, but stories of her mother's plight as a child. Saskia had learned the hard way how to keep her mum talking to her, as she actually seemed to love talking about her journey back into the dark days – and Saskia would always get her mum's best side.

Because she knew just how to appeal to her mother's ego. Her mum would be in her element, as she re-lived a childhood that so needed to be heard and told Saskia of all the awful things that were ready to engulf her as the days moved into her future. One of them was being hit across the face on a regular basis or dragged around by her hair on one occasion; hard, repetitive smacks on her legs, over and over till she screamed out. So, as she grew up, Saskia quickly learned avoidance methods, which she became very sophisticated at. She learned over the years how to work her, how to 'please Mummy'. For example, she realised that her mum's favourite chocolate was Toblerone, so if she saw her mother's mood change, Saskia would scurry around for money and buy it for her. Her mother would smile and say lovely things, and more often than not, there would be no lashing.

One evening she began to tell Saskia – at the tender age of six – about the subject of sex, how she didn't really like it, she found it boring. Saskia misread the meaning behind the story and took it upon herself to make her mother proud of her and have great sex with lots of partners, and most importantly, enjoy it.

'Mummy,' she said wistfully, 'I won't let you down. I'll have lots of sex, I promise.'

'Good for you, sweetheart, you just make sure you do, or it will eat your soul.' Her mother said this with such conviction, having no idea what destructive seeds she had just planted. But Saskia put this on her 'to do list' – the problem being, at six, she thought sex was just kissing.

She was 14 the first time it happened, and she hated it, she trembled all the way through the experience in fear. But nonetheless, the deed had to be done. Her parents were out for the whole day, and she boasted her plan to the boys in her class, who all thought she was the best-looking girl in the whole year: her high cheekbones and blonde hair, perfect white teeth, plus her already good-sized bust. The signs were read incorrectly, though, and were taken advantage of. The girls despised her, but Saskia was clever enough to know what friends to choose, knew the only thing she had done to them was to be beautiful when most of them were ugly ducklings.

Saskia chose her seven favourite boys in her class and invited them back to her house. They all had to take their shoes off at the front door and wait for her command. She went upstairs and stripped naked, and one by one the boys were allowed to come to the bathroom, to look at her naked, touch if they dared or desired. If they wanted to take it further, they had to do it in the bath, so she could wash away the evidence. Not one boy saw her shame or her fear, just her beauty and her sex. Each boy left the bathroom in lust. They all waited for each other down the road to talk endlessly of what had happened. In their eyes, she was now theirs; they owned her. She was an easy slut, no longer a dream but a reality. And that was Saskia's legacy.

What she hadn't anticipated was that her mother would find out eventually from a neighbour.

'I never thought that my daughter would become a slut,' was a difficult thing to hear, but it was too late, it was what she had learned, and forgotten the reason why.

Beauty in a face carved in snow: Saskia wondered how she could bring that face back to life. A joyous glimpse, a twinkle in the eye, she traced the long white beard and el Bandito-style moustache with her hand, and felt the wartime and the cold… She held him in heart, the smile in his eyes held fast within her, and she couldn't help but smile back. This was before his wife's death and before the madness set in.

He lived by a river in a derelict house, he had lived there all his life. When his parents passed away, Jenny moved in, and they had Saskia and Nick. When Saskia was old enough to leave, she was off, but her brother vanished out of their lives at the age of 16. Then his wife committed suicide, and from that moment, the world he knew ceased to exist and everything around him crumbled, he never laid a finger on the house as it tumbled down around him over his next 40 years. He cooked outside, he sat outside on his rickety old chair, smoked his pipe, and lived as close to nature as he could.

Of course, Saskia did try to help her father, and would cry bitterly, but when she looked deep within, she saw he too had passed away from his earthly life. His spirit had carved itself in the surroundings, and he began painting his world in a completely different way.

One particular chilly day, she decided to pay him a visit. He was sitting by his homemade barbecue in his rickety old chair, smoking his pipe. Old empty beer cans surrounded him; paint cans were stacked with car and bike engines, the insides of washing machines, empty plastic buckets going green with age, and piles of wood neatly stacked for his outdoor fire.

She could hear the crackling of the fire and could hear him puffing on his pipe. He looked agitated, had finished his glass of whisky.

'Hello, Pa,' she said carefully so as not to make him jump.

'Huh. What brings you here?'

'I just wanted to make sure you were okay, and that you had everything you need as autumn closes in.'

He turned slowly to face her and scoffed a little more. 'More like you've come to nosey, see if I'm dead yet?'

She sank a little and pulled up an old plastic bucket to perch on. 'Where's Popeye?' Popeye was his dog – she was given that name after her mother bit her in the eye when she was a pup, so her eye protruded. She was a smelly, wiry dog and had been around for many years.

He mumbled under his breath and got up to find a spade. He looked around for a space by the tumbling wall and started digging.

'What are you doing?' she asked, at the same time wishing she hadn't.

He mumbled again; he looked dark and haunted, unlike the bright and sparkling man he once was.

'I'm going to look for Popeye, she usually comes to sit with us by the fire. When did you last see her? She hasn't died, has she?' Saskia felt herself getting more and more upset. As she stood, she gazed into the fire and saw a skull, it looked a bit like the skull of a sheep.

'You've not been killing the farmer's sheep, have you? Don't tell me Popeye killed it.' She put her hand on her forehead, she knew he wouldn't answer. 'Oh my lord, oh my lord.' She stumbled around, looking for the dog.

'Why would I kill the sheep?' he asked angrily. 'That farmer happens to be Doug, my mate, for fuck's sake.' He carried on digging angrily, mumbling as before.

The night started to settle in, and the air fell into a chilly despair. When Saskia noticed a shed made up of tin and wood, she thought better of asking so strolled over to look – maybe Popeye was there. It was a rickety old shed, and she opened the door and called to Popeye, looking for her food bowl. She saw to her horror a mattress and duvet in the middle of the floor, surrounded once again by tin cans and bottles of whisky.

'Is this where you sleep?' she wailed. She decided to leave, this place was unnerving her, and her father looked like a man possessed as he dug furiously.

'Pa, I'm leaving. I'm going to get you some help.'

'Don't you dare, don't you even think about it.'

'And why are you digging that hole in the ground? And where's Popeye? Why are you sleeping in a freezing old shed?'

He stood up, put his spade over his shoulder, and looked at her with seething rage. The next thing she felt was a terrific pain in her neck.

It didn't last. It was over.

The bones were thrown and covered and ignored. The earth dropped its head, and the trees stored the memory, only they had the knowing, only they kept the secret.

THREE WOMEN,
JOURNEYING ONWARDS

The train zoomed through the space between the roots of the trees that hovered above the woodland earth – just enough room for a roaming train. The view from the silver liner was a herd of silvery grey elephants walking their safe pastures of shoreline, coloured up with softest pinks, golds and hazy blues.

The green density on the forest floor lay damp and mossy, the space between was lit up like stars, the space around glowed with life, a life that had been reborn out of suffering into harmony.

So here were three seekers of dreams and visions, all on the train together, all going somewhere together.

All going somewhere…

SERA

Sera found she was struggling to get her breath.

Michael brushed past her and asked if she was okay. 'Take some slow, deep breaths, miss, nice and slow.'

She stared into the density of the vast forest and wondered if she was having allergic reactions. She began to see life reflecting life in the trees, the leaves, the branches. She saw snippets of stories from people's lives, stories that the forest had stored and interpreted. The forest had history in its roots, every last thing recorded, all hidden in the trees.

She heard movement, and as she looked back, she saw a bewildered-looking woman looking frantically around. 'Are you okay?' Sera asked softly.

'Erm, yes, I think so. I'm just wondering where we are going? I'm afraid I'm on the wrong train, I don't recognise where we are.'

Sera stood up and asked the woman to sit awhile and wait for the conductor, who would no doubt help. On reflection, Sera was also a little confused at their whereabouts. It was magnificent scenery, though, a tapestry of colour, and the sun shone down on the treetops and lit her very soul.

The conductor turned up and looked kindly at them both. He seemed in a hurry, but as he swiftly passed, he spoke out loud.

'You want a cup of tea?'

'Yes, I think that would be lovely. I feel icy cold inside, I need warming up.'

'Can I ask your name?' he enquired.

'Of course, how rude of me, it's Jenny.' As the woman finished her sentence, she exhaled very slowly, her breath looked like a cloud of smoke that seemed to permeate the whole of the carriage.

'We need to warm you up, Jenny. I'll get that tea.' He looked at Sera, who was looking at this stranger. 'One for you too, miss.'

INDIA

India felt lost in time and space, it was a little alarming. She felt a wave of energy behind her, but as she gazed back, there was nothing in her vision, just a freeing feeling.

Gardens, temples and castles were in the scenery outside the windows of the train. Magnificent ones. India felt sick; she was moving forward, but felt a pull back, then nausea. She sipped her Golden Rod tea, the colour of yellow okra lit by the sun, and wondered if it was that giving her the uncontrolled need to throw up… She reached the toilet at just the right time.

Returning, India saw a female figure sitting beneath a tree in the distance, feeding the swans, swans of white and silver, which was blinding. Beside them was another female figure in a pink flamingo dress, burning hot flamingo pink. India found herself smiling, and the sick feeling disappeared.

A memory surfaced from a wave of energy coming from the past, conjuring a male figure with piercing black eyes – almost terrestrial and elemental at the same time. His feet were points, as were his hands. She saw him in the dark green, frightening her on a very deep level, as he arrived through an opening her father had made. This figure had often edged through what looked like the eye of a needle and taunted India for years. He would jab around her dreams and sew up her veins so she couldn't breathe, her breath would tighten, her body would tighten and then he'd just let go, as fast as he had held on. India woke up coughing and gasping for breath, and her father told her she had allergies. This, the dark green lord found very amusing, as of course, he was the allergy brought on by her father. India always felt strongly she would die in her slumber, no one to help, suffocating at the mercy of the elemental allergy.

She shot up out of her seat – she needed to move, or she'd cry. Already her nose dripped instead of tears, and it felt like acid drops. She fled to the next carriage, looking a little wild, wild as a lone wolf in need of its pack. She saw two women drinking tea. They smiled at her, she smiled back.

'I'm Sera and this is Jenny,' one of them said.

'I'm India,' she replied in a shivery voice.

Sera saw the reflection of the wolf twice now, and somehow knew to get the inner fire lit. She asked India if she was okay and watched as India made some strange movements; her words had escaped her for a minute. 'Here, sit and feel the warmth of that huge sun from outside,' she said.

India's skin got back its pink hue, and each of them felt the warmth and the feeling of life once again.

All three looked up at once and saw another woman walking quickly through the carriage. She was chasing a dog.

'Thorne? Oh, wow!' India sat up, totally aghast. 'Thorne, you're here. How did you get here?'

She looked at the new woman, who explained, 'I'm Saskia. I was just sitting in my seat and that dog came to me, looking happy and wanting some fuss. Just as I leaned forward, she headed off into the next carriage. Here. I wanted to make sure she was okay.'

India's eyes shone. 'This is Thorne, everyone. I'm so happy she's here, she's my baby.'

With that, the conductor strolled through the carriage again, carrying what looked to be an e-cigarette. He appeared to be blowing smoke of many colours.

'I see we haven't got too far to go now,' he said. He looked at Jenny specifically and told her not to worry as she was on the correct train and to sit back and enjoy her tea. As he spoke, the smoke turned into letters, and the letters into words, and they repeated his last sentence in the space behind.

The eyeless face, the speechless speaker. The face that can only see with inner vision, and a mouth to utter the words. India saw it clear as clay, as if it was moulded and thrown onto an old tin roof. She looked three times before she got the message. Messages of insight, inner sight surging into the abyss for anything new to be found. Mist and gold, angels and feathers, mulberry glowing in the ice, the eyes, the brow furrowed, down deep in solace… where birth and death resided, where love and hate held hands… where all sat… kill and be killed… live and soar through the valley of your soul… choice and choice…

India had decided to meet the man in the wood. She often saw him with his stick as he strolled in the morning with his dog, and she made her acquaintance carefully by purposefully pausing and giving out a happy good morning. The next time, she made sure she walked towards him, once again with a happy good morning. This went on for a while, till one day the dog came to her for some attention.

She looked then at the bearded man, full of wonder, believing in the light she saw behind his eyes – light that was so bright she didn't spy the dark flame, she saw only good in this man. She patted the dog excitedly and mentioned the weather, talked about her own dog and how the two of them would be running all over the place by now. He just stood and grunted, then took his leave.

The next day she brought her dog – Thorne. She felt the man was lonely, there was a deep sorrow that he carried, but there was also something else she couldn't quite put her finger on. As time went by, they talked more, and he seemed to soften, he seemed to like India. One day they discussed art, they both loved painting, and before India could control herself, she had agreed to go back to his house and look at his work.

India met him by the river and strolled along the path to the tin and wooden hut, where he offered her a bucket to perch on. She noted the fire embers settling to the ground that had been burned over and over, she noted the tin roof, and she felt uneasy. She saw the cans and the bottles and the piles of wood, engines, and sticks; it was all closing in on her, and she called for her dog. The man sat in his chair and said nothing, he just lit his pipe and looked toward her, where he spied fear. It fitted her like a cape – she was speechless as the fear rooted into her and felt unable to move, the roots grabbed her ankles, and slowly this intriguing kindly old man became menacing, right there in front of her. She looked for help, but saw only darkness, and she felt the earth move in on her, speaking of birth and death. India's breath became more and more shallow, her blood ran through into the earth, finding a new place to be, weight covered her, heavy weight and unfamiliar bones. Even as she felt the presence of death, the presence of life took hold, and out of the ground she came. Into the light of the trees she flew, where she waited a while in the treetops, and there she was met by gentleness and love.

THEIR JOURNEY'S END

The conductor arrived with cherry pie and a cheery note. 'Just to let you ladies know, we are just pulling into the station for one last pick up, then it's not far to go after that.'

The train stopped quite suddenly, without the feeling of slowing down; there was just stillness. A very crippled old man boarded, he held a stick, had a long white beard, and his eyes looked ahead though he saw no one. The conductor sat him down next to the women, who stared in horror.

Saskia could see the cold frosty breath coming from his mouth; India could see roots around his ankles dragging him down; Sera could see that blackberry black in his eyes; Jenny saw a man possessed.

'Is anyone here?' he sobbed. 'I'm blind, I'm confused, I've been on a long and terrible journey. It's been cold, so very cold, the frost has got into me, I think I'm dying.'

The women looked at each other, deathly quiet. Their minds were numb for a moment.

Jenny was the first to speak. 'Andrew, is that you?' She reached over to him and took his gnarled rooted hand, and she gently rubbed the coldness to give warmth. A tear found its way down the passages in his face, but he said nothing. Jenny got closer and saw into his mulberry blackberry eyes, she saw way back, and there he was at the other side, the youth she had fallen in love with all those years ago. 'Andrew, Andrew... I'm here,' she said. 'Your wife. It's Jenny...' She looked up at the frozen faces of the other women, alarmed that everyone was still and silent.

No one really knew what to say. In fact, no one really knew anything – why they were all together on the same train, or where they were going... Fear began to penetrate like poison around them, at which point Michael, our conductor – their guardian – arrived on the scene. He spoke kindly and gently of a new world where they could all reside, of the vast possibilities ahead. He spoke of shorelines and whispers of forgiveness, new beginnings and learning, knowledge and wisdom, great mirrors, great cathedrals, entrances to new galaxies...

Once that tear, his tear, had spilled, new life began to grow and blossom with such beauty. The women saw in him their murderer, and the realisation of their deaths began to penetrate.

The women watched the path that one tear took, watched as it fell gently and fiercely into everyone's heart, where it stayed and shook the worlds within the worlds of every cell of their spirit. Each one looked up, and their eyes were a little more colourful.

The fire burned a little warmer; like the sun, it took hold of hearts and souls, and a gentle ease began to take hold of all these women.

The shell of this man, Andrew, grew more and more rigid, starting around his throat. He was angry, and the roots of hellish thoughts began to pull on every sinew. He felt a thud, the sort of thud you feel on an elevator that stops on your floor.

The madness in his mind became fuelled with fear, and he felt again his hands around the fragile necks of his victims. He hung them by ropes around the branches of his antlers like prizes, he could smell the rot setting in, and then he could hear the haunting chimes of bones rattling victoriously.

He had killed them all again: Sera, India, Saskia – and yes, even Jenny. He had completely forgotten about the love he once had for this woman, because somehow her vulnerability became an inward spiral that inspired his demons rather than tamed his mental trust and torture.

These four women on the train watched the tormented soul as his throat rattled, they saw his demise, they saw his madness, they watched him suffocate on himself, they saw him crack like an eggshell and watched him fall into decay.

As he shattered, Janthi was waiting in the woodland for his fall. She had prepared a cocoon of silk to comfort his wounded self, to wrap him so gently in peace to ease his rotten heart and leave him there until the day he decided to live again, to set himself free from his own destruction and his own self-hatred. She surrounded him with herbs from her garden – her garden was her paradise, her love and her soul. She had created a protective field for his illness by using her ground and her lightness. She would visit him often, along with many other tormented souls waiting for their resurrection, their birth once again. Nobody, no soul was left forgotten, even when they forget themselves.

The women were resurrected on this train. They were set free from earthly shackles, they broke free and were ready to fly, fly into the unknown realms of worlds untold.

Michael was standing at the door beaming, beckoning them to leave, showing them the lighted way. As they looked up and beyond, they saw a golden lit gateway, and there was great joy in the hearts of the living.

They didn't remember leaving the train.

Lightning Source UK Ltd.
Milton Keynes UK
UKHW050835120921
390335UK00004B/38

9 781839 756054